Bakery

Graggar House

Costume Factory

Purimville

Graggar Fields

Meadow

Sarah & Jacob
← arrive here

PROBLEMS IN

Purimville

- A PURIM STORY -

For JJ and Rachel,
for whom anything is possible.

Other books in the series:
An Adventure in Latkaland

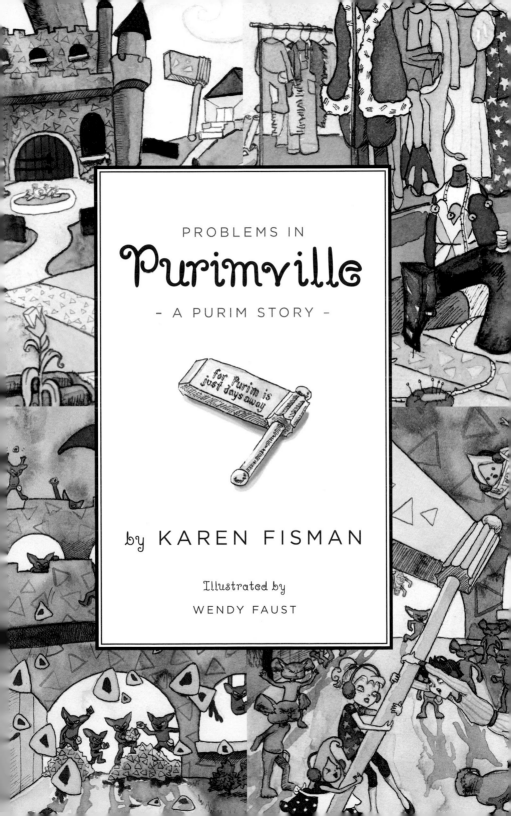

PROBLEMS IN

Purimville

- A PURIM STORY -

for Purim is just days away

by KAREN FISMAN

Illustrated by
WENDY FAUST

Library and Archives Canada Cataloguing in Publication
Fisman, Karen, 1965-
Problems in Purimville : a Purim story /
Karen Fisman ; illustrated by Wendy Faust.

ISBN 978-0-9812650-1-8
I. Faust, Wendy, 1978- II. Title.

PS8611.I85P76 2010
jC813'.6   C2010-904302-2

Printed in Canada

TABLE OF CONTENTS

CHAPTER
1
A Crazy Morning

One snowy, grey morning in February, Jacob woke up with a jolt. He'd been dreaming of the adventure he'd had last Hanukkah with a girl named Sarah. In his dream, he and Sarah were leading an army of brave fighters against a horde of evil goblins. But all of a sudden, the brave fighters had turned into hamantashen - triangle shaped Purim cookies. Then the hamantashen grew arms and legs and began to sing and dance! That was when Jacob woke up.

He supposed that with Purim just a day away, it was no surprise he was dreaming about hamantashen, even singing, dancing ones. Jacob couldn't wait until the holiday, when he and his friends would all dress up in fantastic costumes and parade to synagogue to hear the Purim story. The story told of how, long ago in the faraway land of Persia, brave Queen Esther and her Uncle Mordecai saved the Jewish people from a nasty villain named Haman. Whenever Haman's name was spoken, everyone would spin noisy rattles called graggers to drown out the evil sound. It was pretty deafening, but really fun!

Jacob planned to dress up as a king this year. He thought about his costume and suddenly felt like trying it on again. He took the costume bag from his closet and opened it, but as he shook out its contents, he frowned. This was all wrong. The bag should have contained a jewel studded crown, a blue velvet cloak and a very cool sword and shield (which his mom said he wasn't allowed to bring to synagogue). Instead, out of the bag came a pink tutu, a pair of purple and green flippers, and disguise glasses – the kind with a large plastic nose and mustache. What was going on here?

Jacob left the muddled up costume on his bed and went downstairs to the kitchen. He thought maybe his mom or dad was playing a trick on him. The kitchen was empty, but there was a note from his mom on the counter.

"Jacob, I'll be back soon. If you need anything, ask dad – he's still upstairs. There are some hamantashen for you on the kitchen counter. Since Purim is coming soon, you can have them for breakfast, for a treat. They're your favourite – poppy seed."

"Awesome," thought Jacob, as he spied the cookies that were shaped like the wicked Haman's triangular hat. He forgot for the moment about his costume problem and helped himself to a hamantash. It looked delicious

– slightly golden cookie dough on the outside folded around a dark, gooey centre. He took a large bite and…*Blech! Ptooey!* He spat it out.

The hamantash tasted bitter and spicy at the same time - like it was filled with brussels sprouts and sprinkled with hot chili sauce. He tossed the leftover on the counter and dashed to the fridge for some orange juice to take the awful taste away. Something was very wrong, he thought to himself as he poured. First the mixed-up costume, and now the mixed-up hamantash. What was going to happen next?

As Jacob gulped down his last bit of juice, the doorbell rang. He hurried to the door and peered through the glass. There, on the front step, was his friend Sarah. In the months since their Hanukkah adventure, Sarah had been living just around the corner with her Uncle Solomon. She'd often drop by for a visit, but today something seemed different. Sarah looked like she was about to burst with excitement. Jacob opened the door, and she dashed into the house.

"I have something really crazy to show you," Sarah said breathlessly. "You're not going to believe your eyes."

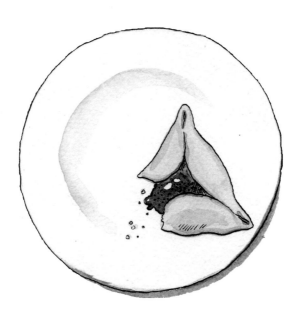

2

A Call for Help

Sarah whipped off her coat and shot up the stairs. "Come on," she called over her shoulder, and Jacob raced up behind her.

They went to Jacob's room and closed the door. "What's going on?" he asked, bursting with curiosity.

"Look at this," said Sarah. She dumped the contents of her knapsack onto Jacob's bed. "Yesterday, my Uncle Solomon and I went to get me a costume. I was going to be Queen Esther, so I got a crown, queen's gown, scepter – you know, what you'd expect. But look here.

When I opened the costume bag this morning, I found these." She swept her arm over the items, which included floppy donkey's ears and a large stuffed pumpkin costume in a brilliant shade of orange.

"This is really weird, Sarah," said Jacob. "Have a look here." He showed Sarah his tutu and flippers. "The same thing happened to me."

"Yeah, very weird," agreed Sarah thoughtfully, then added, "But that's not all." Reaching into a side pocket of her knapsack, she pulled out something shining and gold. Jacob stared at the object. It was a rectangular golden box, its surface radiant, almost alive, and sparkling with light. The box was attached to a small cylindrical handle. It looked just like a gragger, a Purim noisemaker. But never in Jacob's eight years had he seen a gragger like this one.

"Where did you get that?" he asked, feeling prickles of excitement.

"It *was* my Latkaland coin," said Sarah. "I checked on it this morning and found this in its place. Get yours - see if it's changed as well."

At the end of their Hanukkah adventure, Jacob and Sarah had each received a gold coin as a gift of thanks from the little creatures of Latkaland. Jacob dashed over to his closet and reached to the very back of the shelf where he kept his coin. But it wasn't there. In its place was a rectangular box, a box on a handle…just like Sarah's. He pulled it out. And sure enough, there in his hand was a golden gragger.

"What does this mean?" Jacob wondered out loud. As if in answer, words suddenly appeared on the gragger's shining surface:

"Your help is needed, don't delay,
In Purimville, so far away,
Where costumes are precisely sewn
And fields of gragger plants are grown,
Where hamantashen baked with care
Make scrumptious smells that fill the air.
There is a problem now you see
A problem that's a mystery.
The costumes have become so muddled,
Purimville is quite befuddled.
Please come quickly, don't delay
For Purim is just days away!"

The last words faded, leaving just the twinkling, golden surface behind.

"Hmmm," said Sarah, "It sounds like someone needs our help again – and fast."

"Yeah," said Jacob, "In Purimville. But how, exactly, do we get ourselves to Purimville?"

In answer to Jacob's question, a new message immediately appeared on his gragger. This one was less polite, but still in rhyme. Jacob read it out loud.

"It's Purim, get it, use your head!
What d'ya do when Haman's name is said?"

"Um…we make lots of noise?" suggested Jacob, feeling a bit odd talking to a gragger, even if it was a golden, magical one.

"Yeah, we make noise with our graggers," added Sarah, excitedly. "And that must be how we get to Purimville." She raised her gragger, ready to rattle. "Come on, Jacob, let's give it a try."

Jacob suddenly felt knots twisting and tugging at the pit of his stomach. He didn't know *what* they would find in Purimville, and that was scary, but he did really want another adventure. He took a deep breath and raised his gragger. "Okay," he said to Sarah, his voice just a tiny bit shaky, "Let's get to Purimville!"

3

The Adventure Begins

acob and Sarah clasped hands tightly and spun their graggers, first slowly, then faster and faster. The graggers produced a satisfying rattle, getting louder with each spin. Brilliant sparks flew, forcing the children to close their eyes against the brightness.

They sensed a change in the air around them, suddenly feeling the warmth of a gentle breeze, and smelling the faint aroma of freshly baked cookies. The gragger's rattle began to slow to a dull clackety-clack, then stopped altogether.

The children opened their eyes, blinking hard against sunlight that now shone from a peacock blue sky. They looked around. They were standing in the middle of a green meadow scattered here and there with patches of colourful flowers.

Suddenly, there was movement across the meadow. Something very odd was scampering towards them, huffing and puffing like a little steam engine. The Something was shaped like a triangle with the flat part at the bottom and wore a smudgy white apron over a frilly smock the colour of strawberry jam. When it reached the children, the Something drew to a halt, gasping for breath. Extracting a very large handkerchief from an apron pocket, it mopped droplets of sweat from its triangular face, all the while peering at the children with two anxious (but kindly) round eyes.

"Oh my!" it exclaimed in a rather high-pitched voice, sounding much more like a she than a he. "I haven't run like that in years. Thank goodness you've finally arrived! I've been waiting for ages."

"We came as soon as we got the message," Sarah explained calmly. "But who are you…and how did you know about us?"

"My good friend Oily in Latkaland told me all about you. You must be Jacob," she said to Sarah, "And you must be Sarah," she said to Jacob.

Jacob gulped. "Other way round," he muttered.

The creature blushed a strawberry red that matched her smock. "Oh dear, I have such trouble telling humans apart."

"That's okay," said Sarah, "but please, do tell us who you are and why you called us here?"

"My name is Poppy," the creature said in a firmer tone. "I'm a hamantashy – just like everyone else here in Purimville – except *I* am the hamantashy leader. And I called you here because we hamantashies are facing a horrible, hapless, hamanish problem." Poppy paused and shuddered at the thought.

"Um…excuse me Poppy, but what is this… um…horrible, hamanish problem, exactly?" asked Jacob.

"Oh, yes, of course. Well, when you were back home, before you came to Purimville, did you notice anything that seemed a little strange… maybe with your Purim costumes or some hamantashen that you tasted?"

"We did!" cried the children, in unison.

"Mm hm," Poppy nodded her pointy head. "Well, you see, the costumes you wear, the graggers you rattle, even the hamantashen you eat on Purim – many of them are made right here in Purimville. Our Purimville products are quite marvelous – until this year, there's never been a complaint. But just recently, we've learned our delicious hamantashen are arriving in your world tasting quite revolting, and our wonderful costumes are becoming mixed up and muddled."

"What about the graggers?" asked Jacob.

"For some reason, there's no problem at all with the graggers," said Poppy, then added glumly, "The whole thing is really quite mysterious. We have absolutely no idea who or what is behind this troublesome mess."

"Hmmm," Sarah looked thoughtful. Then she turned to the hamantashy. "For starters, Poppy, why don't you show us around Purimville, and we'll look for clues that might help us solve your mysterious problem."

ૠ

A Purimville Tour

The children followed Poppy along a narrow path paved with stones that glittered like gems in the sunlight. They passed alongside vast chocolate brown fields dotted here and there with rather odd looking plants. Each plant had a short stalk topped with pale, rectangular fruit that twirled round and around in the gentle breeze.

"Those are our gragger fields," said Poppy. "Most of the graggers have already been harvested but as you can see, there are still a few left in the ground."

"They don't look like the graggers *we* use on Purim," observed Jacob.

"Of course not," said Poppy. "Those are gragger *plants*. They still have to be dried and decorated, then you'd recognize them." She took a sharp turn to the left and beckoned to the children. "This way, please."

They rounded the corner and the path ended abruptly, opening onto a courtyard that was bustling with activity. Hamantashies scurried here and there. Some were dressed like bakers while others wielded scissors and pin cushions, and yet others were smudged with paint, and wore very large earmuffs on their pointy heads. They all looked terribly busy, and didn't seem to even notice Poppy and the children.

At the front of the courtyard, there was a long building dotted from bottom to top with an array of painted hamantashen.

"That must be the bakery," said Sarah.

"Actually, it's our costume factory." Poppy chuckled. "We like to mix things up a bit in Purimville. The bakery's just over there. Come, have a look inside." She headed towards a second building which looked like a small, exotic palace – but nothing at all like a bakery. It had a turreted roof and walls of deep purple that sparkled with silvery glitter.

The children followed Poppy and peered in through one of the bakery's arched windows, breathing in the rich, wonderful aroma of freshly baked cookies. Inside, hamantashies were very busy at work. They rolled dough, made dozens of different fillings, and slid trays of hamantashen into two enormous ovens to bake. A crew of rather roundish tasters tested the cookies when they were done, then placed them carefully into boxes.

"It doesn't look like anything's wrong here," remarked Sarah to Poppy.

"I know." Poppy sighed. "It's all just fine when we pack up at the end of the day – here and at the costume factory. And everything's shipped off first thing in the morning. So where could it possibly be going wrong?"

"Whoever's messing with your stuff must be doing it at night, then," suggested Jacob.

Poppy nodded her head. "That does make sense. You see, each night after our work is done, we frolic in the gragger house, over there." She pointed beyond the bakery at a third building with thick, windowless walls and an enormous gragger standing guard in front of the heavy door. "Hamantashies love frolicking so everyone attends, even during these difficult times. The gragger house is completely soundproofed, so we wouldn't hear anything outside. And anything outside wouldn't hear us."

Sarah's eyes suddenly lit up, the way they did when she had a plan. "Okay then. Tonight, while the hamantashies are frolicking, *we* will keep watch by the bakery and find out just what is going on."

5

Trouble at the Bakery

That night, Poppy and the children positioned themselves behind a bushy shrub near one of the bakery windows. They watched from their hiding place as a glittering parade of hamantashies passed by, heading towards the gragger house for their evening frolic. There were hamantashy kings and queens, villains and superheroes, and at the tail end, a bulging, brilliant orange hamantashy pumpkin, her pointed head trailing vines of leafy green.

As the last hamantashy vanished around the corner, the trio settled down to wait. The sky turned black, lit by a round silver moon, and silence hung heavily over Purimville.

"Perhaps the meddlers won't come tonight," Poppy whispered hopefully. "Perhaps they've had word that the two of you are here, and that's that.

Perhaps we should just go and join the frolic."

"Shhhh, Poppy," chided Sarah. "The night's just begun. We've got to give it some time." And no sooner had she spoken, than all three heard a noise – a distinct rustling from the other side of the bakery.

The trio crept stealthily to the bakery window and peered in. By the light of the moon, they could see right through the large window on the opposite side. And something was definitely there. "I think it's just more hamantashies," whispered Jacob, squinting at the shadowy shapes. "I guess they're late for the frolic."

"Oh no they're not," said Poppy, her voice a little shaky. "Because one thing I know for sure about hamantashies – hamantashies *do not fly!*"

They peered through the window. Poppy was right. Whoever was on the other side of the bakery had to be hovering several feet in the air! Suddenly, there was a flurry of movement and the shadowy shapes flattened themselves out then slid inside, right through a crack at the bottom of the window. An eerie light lit up the bakery as the mysterious creatures landed feet first on the floor and blew themselves back up like little grey balloons.

The creatures were about hamantashy size, but everything else was completely different - from their spindly grey bodies to their remarkably large pointed ears, bulging eyes, and wide, mischievous mouths. "What are they?" wondered Jacob, his voice a bit shaky.

"I know what they are," murmured Poppy, fearfully. "They're shape shifters – most often called gremlins. I've never seen them before, but I've heard stories, bad stories, and I can tell you this. Gremlins love to make wicked trouble, and they'll use nasty tricks on anyone who tries to stop them."

CHAPTER

6

Gremlins!

Inside the bakery, the gremlins skittered gleefully over to the carefully packed boxes of hamantashen and opened every last one. Then they reached into silver pouches that hung at their waists and took out small spray bottles. Waggling their enormous ears, the gremlins rose like a storm cloud into the air, hovered over the hamantashen and began to spray. As they sprayed, their wide mouths stretched into wicked whoops and giggles. Oddly, however, the whoops and giggles were completely silent.

Each gremlin's bottle had a tiny picture on it. Jacob could see images of brussels sprouts and hot chili sauce. "That's what ruined my poppy seed hamantash," he whispered to Sarah. They looked on, horrified, as gremlins sprayed rotten egg, moldy cheese, spoiled sardine and other revolting flavours all over the hamantashen. These nasty pests had to be stopped, but how?

All of a sudden, Poppy gave a loud, angry yelp. The children turned, just in time to see her making a dash for the bakery door. "Poppy, wait! Where are you going?" Jacob cried.

"Must…do…something," Poppy huffed and puffed over her shoulder, without slowing down the least bit. "Wicked…creatures…must…stop…now." Jacob shot a worried glance at Sarah, and together, they tore after Poppy.

"Wait Poppy!" shouted Sarah breathlessly, as they ran. "Remember, you said gremlins could be really nasty."

But it was too late. Just as the children caught up, Poppy reached the bakery and with a swift push of the door, burst inside. Without wasting a moment, she scolded in a fierce voice (or at least as fierce as a hamantashy's voice can be): "Stop it this instant, you wicked, horrible pests. Just get out of Purimville - and don't ever, ever come back!"

At the sound of Poppy's shrill cry, the gremlins thudded to the ground like stones. They stuck their long grey fingers into their enormous ears, which immediately closed up tight, like some flowers do at night. Then, the gremlins puffed up their cheeks and blew, and with that blowing came a great wooshing wind that lifted Jacob, Sarah and Poppy way up into the air and sent them hurtling backwards, right out of the bakery. The doors slammed shut behind them, and the wind abruptly stopped. The trio dropped with a thud, landing in a heap on top of a leafy bush.

Jacob found himself sandwiched between Sarah and Poppy. He was winded, but thankfully, okay. "Ged uphh!" he called in a muffled voice to Sarah, who was at the top of the heap. She rolled off and Jacob was able to stumble to his feet. He offered a hand to Poppy, who had been at the bottom of the pile and was looking quite stunned and a little bit flatter.

"Whatever are we going to do?" cried Poppy, as she clambered to her feet, brushing dirt and leaves from her smudgy apron. "If we try to stop them, they'll just blow us away – next time, maybe right out of Purimville altogether."

"There's not going to be a next time, Poppy," said Sarah. "And we *are* going to stop them. Come on, let's think. What do we know so far?"

"Well for starters," offered Jacob, "Gremlins don't seem to make any noise at all. Even when they were whooping and giggling in the bakery, they were completely quiet."

"And remember," added Sarah, "When Poppy burst into the bakery and yelled at the gremlins, they closed their ears up tight."

"Yeah, those crazy huge ears," said Jacob, his eyes suddenly bright. "You know what? I think gremlins really don't like noise. And I'd guess they're probably pretty scared of it." The other two nodded excitedly.

"That would be why they never ever mess with our graggers," said Poppy. "Because Purimville graggers are frightfully noisy."

"That makes sense," said Sarah. "But if we're going to use noise to get rid of the gremlins, we need to find something so loud they can't block it out. And I don't know what that could be."

"It's quite obvious to me!" exclaimed Poppy. "We can use graggers, of course. We have hundreds of freshly dried graggers over in the gragger house. And hundreds of frolicking hamantashies in there as well. If each hamantashy rattles a gragger, all at the same time, it should make quite a horrifying racket."

"Good thinking," said Jacob, giving Poppy's shoulder a pat. "Let's go and get ourselves some noisemakers!"

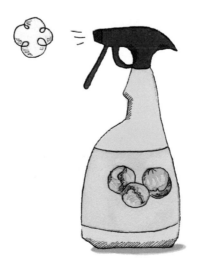

7

At the Frolic

Poppy and the children hurried off towards the gragger house. They passed beneath the giant flagpole, and stopped before the heavy door. Poppy grasped the door handle, and with a small grunt, pulled it open, releasing a blast of noise, song, and general merriment into the silent night.

The children stepped through the doorway and looked around. Hamantashies were everywhere, most in full costume, though assorted headpieces, cloaks, and a trailing pumpkin vine scattered the floor. There were hamantashies lounging on chairs, swigging goblets of rich, chocolaty-looking liquid and cheering as others performed tricks on the work tables or swung a bit dangerously from the light fixtures. But most of the hamantashies were merrily singing and dancing in one of several large circles in the centre of the work room. The song that they were singing went something like this:

(sung to the tune of Hag Purim)

"Hamantash, hamantash
Scrumptious yummy tasty nosh.
Poppy seed, chocolate too,
Got one just for you

Chorus:

Mix up the dough and pat, pat, pat;
Make it a shape like Haman's hat.
Bake it until it's golden brown.
Best hamantash in town. HEY!!!!!!"

After the loud *"HEY!"*, the song would start over again, getting faster and faster until all the dancers eventually collapsed in a great giggling heap on the floor.

Jacob gaped at the chaotic scene. "How are we ever going to get these hamantashies to listen to us?"

"I know what to do," said Sarah, dashing to the lone work table that was free of somersaulting hamantashies. She vaulted onto the table and gave a piercing whistle that somehow sliced through the ruckus, stopping the hamantashies in their frolicking tracks.

There were a few seconds of silence followed by puzzled chatter.

"Who did that?"

"Look – over there."

(Really impressed murmur) "Wow…who is she, and how does she whistle like that. Maybe she'll teach me."

Sarah held up her hands, and there was silence. She beckoned to Jacob and Poppy, who climbed onto the table beside her.

"Hamantashies," Sarah began, in that calm, confident voice she used when things got a bit tough, "Your leader, Poppy, called on us - Jacob and me - to help solve your Purimville problem. We've learned that it's gremlins messing with your delicious hamantashan and amazing costumes, and those gremlins are in the bakery at this very moment! We do know how to stop them, but we need *your* help."

There was a collective gasp.

"Gremlins – the wicked trickster kind?"

"Ooooooh…this is very scary!"

"What will we do?!"

"Hamantashies, listen," said Jacob loudly. "Sarah and I chased the goblins out of Latkaland and with your help, we *will* chase the gremlins from Purimville." There was a pause in the worried chatter, and Jacob quickly continued. "Gremlins don't like noise, so we're going to make lots of it. You'll each need a gragger – maybe even two. Then we'll march very quietly to the bakery and take those Purim spoilers by surprise."

"We'll show those gremlins!" came a shrill cry from the back.

"Yeah, let's go get noisy!" came another. And the hamantashies dashed off to arm themselves with noisemakers.

"Don't forget your earmuffs, everyone," called Poppy anxiously. Then she hopped off the table and disappeared into the crowd, returning shortly with three graggers and three pairs of earmuffs – one set for her and one for each of the children.

Jacob and Sarah put on their earmuffs. And just in time, as the hamantashies were now busy testing how much noise they could make – which happened to be a great deal!

Then Sarah gave a whistle that pierced the rattling racket. The hamantashies stopped whirling their graggers and everyone removed their earmuffs.

"Hamantashies, line up," ordered Sarah. "No more noise until we get to the bakery – and then, only when we see the bad guys. Just like when you hear Haman's name on Purim. My whistle's the signal, okay?"

Pointed hamantashy heads bobbed up and down in agreement.

"Come on, everyone, let's march," called Jacob. Then Poppy heaved open the gragger house door. With the children in the lead, the ear-muffed, gragger bearing hamantashies marched silently towards the bakery, through the still, dark night.

8

The Great Battle

After the rowdiness of the frolic, Jacob was amazed at how quiet the hamantashies could be. Once at the bakery, they stealthily circled the building, then waited for Sarah's signal to launch the noise attack.

Jacob counted down on his fingers: three, two, one...then Sarah whistled - *Phweeeeeeeeet!* And the graggers rattled.

The gremlins were taken by surprise. They plummeted to the ground, some knocked flat on their backs by the noise. But then, just like before, their large, pointed ears rapidly sealed up tight, and they got to their feet and huddled in the centre of the bakery. Jacob looked worriedly at Sarah, who pointed to her gragger, and rattled it more vigorously than ever.

But it wasn't enough. The gremlins broke from their huddle, wicked grins stretching from tightly sealed ear to ear. A few of them headed to the bakery windows and door, while the rest moved towards the boxes of hamantashen. Suddenly, the windows and door were flung wide open. *And then there was chaos!*

From inside the bakery, through every opening, a shower of hamantashen came flying, pelting hamantashies and children, splatting like little stink bombs as they hit their marks. Graggers dropped to the ground and earmuffs were abandoned as hamantashies fled, helter skelter, from the smelly scene. Jacob flinched as a hamantash hit him squarely on the forehead. Filling trickled down his nose, and he smelled something like moldy cheese mixed with a bit of poppy seed. He pulled off his earmuffs, grabbed Sarah and Poppy, and altogether, they ran back towards the gragger factory, ducking the hamantashen that continued to fly overhead.

When they were out of range, they stopped, panting for breath and wiping the stinky filling off their faces and clothes. "This is so disgusting," said Sarah, as she wiped a glob of cherry coloured goop off her chin. "I don't know if I'll ever be able to eat a hamantash again."

"Oh, don't say that," whimpered Poppy, wringing her hands in despair.

Jacob drew his sleeve across his face, wiping away the moldy filling that mixed with a few disappointed tears. He sighed. "I guess we were wrong," he said to Poppy and Sarah. "Noise won't get rid of the gremlins – they just block it out."

"Come on, Jacob," said Sarah, "Don't give up. We were right about the noise. I'm sure of it! We've just got to find something louder." Then her eyes lit up, and she pointed towards the gragger house. "Over there," she said, "*that's* our noisemaker!"

9

A Noisy Ending

Jacob and Poppy turned and looked. Sarah was pointing to the giant gragger that towered in front of the gragger house.

"Does it work?" she asked Poppy.

Poppy nodded her head. "Oh yes. It's the largest gragger ever grown in Purimville history. It's dangerously loud – the hamantashies that painted it were deaf for months after. We decided it wouldn't do at all for children to use on Purim, even though it would have done a wonderful job at drowning out Haman's name. So it's stayed here, in front of the gragger house all these years.

"Can we use it, Poppy?" asked Jacob, hopeful that the noise plan might work after all.

"We can try," Poppy said, then eyed her fellow hamantashies, who were scurrying rapidly away from the bakery battle scene, and added, "But we'll need some extra help, and I'm not sure how we're going to get it."

"Leave that to me," said Sarah and ran off, returning minutes later with a length of silver cord that could only have come from the costume factory. She fashioned the cord into a giant lasso which she twirled above her head and dropped over a pack of fleeing hamantashies, stopping them abruptly in their tracks.

Sarah hurried over to the scared little group and loosened the lasso while she did some explaining. Once she had calmed them, she called to Jacob and Poppy. "I've explained what we're going to do," she said, then smiled her reassuring smile at the hamantashies. "And you're going to be very brave and help us, aren't you?"

There was nervous nodding all around.

"Okay then, let's go," said Jacob, and they trooped to the front of the gragger house and unlatched the giant noise maker from its stand. Moving the gragger was no easy feat, but somehow they managed, slowly lowering it so it could be carried like a giant log. It took Jacob, Sarah, Poppy and a dozen hamantashies to transport the gragger. There was plenty of grumbling and mumbling from the hamantashies, who, as a rule, were not used to carrying heavy loads, but they did get to the bakery quite quickly. Then they raised the gragger back up and latched it firmly into position just beside one of the doors, where it couldn't be seen.

Jacob and Sarah peeked stealthily through a window. The bakery was splattered and smeared with ruined hamantashen and the gremlins were gathered together in the centre of the floor.

"Looks like they're getting ready to go," Sarah reported in a whisper. "I bet they're heading to the costume factory next. Let's wait for them all to get outside, then we'll blast them with noise." Everyone nodded their agreement. *"Here they come."*

Children and hamantashies crouched in the shadows as the horde of horrid pointy eared gremlins smirked and sniggled their way out through the bakery door. But then, just as the last creature exited the bakery, one of the hamantashies gave a loud, nervous hiccup. Jacob held his breath, hoping the gremlins wouldn't notice, but of course, they did! Large pointed ears started waggling quite madly, and gnarled hairy paws pointed in their direction.

Jacob leapt to his feet. "Quickly," he called, "Earmuffs on and let's rattle!" Out of the corner of his eye, he could see the gremlins' cheeks puffing up. If they blew a gust of wind, the plan would be ruined. Jacob, Sarah and the hamantashies might be blown so far from Purimville that all would be lost for good.

Jacob pulled his earmuffs over his ears and dashed to the base of the gragger with Sarah and the hamantashies on his heels. As quickly as they could, they began to rock the pole of the gragger back and forth, willing the great rattle to start spinning. But just then, the first gust of gremlin wind hit. Jacob hung on tight to the gragger pole, feeling his feet lift right off the ground. Hamantashies tumbled past him through the air, but he could see Sarah and Poppy hanging on with all their might, and he continued to do the same.

The wind picked up and Jacob could see some of the gremlins grinning their wicked grins as they blew. Then, just as he was beginning to feel like he couldn't hang on for another second, there was a resounding boom. The boom repeated again and again, getting faster and louder until, even through his earmuffs, it sounded like a deafening volley of cannon blasts. It was the giant gragger, of course. The gremlins, with their enormous gusts of wind, had started the rattle spinning!

Jacob felt a surge of strength, and he clung to the gragger pole tighter than ever, feet flying parallel to the ground. With a mighty effort,

he lifted his head to check out the gremlins...
and what a surprise he got! The strangest thing
was happening to them. Of course, they'd shut
up their ears, trying to block out the enormous
sound, but this time it wasn't working. The
giant gragger was too loud and they were too
close by. Like a glass exposed to just the right
type of sound, the gremlins vibrated back and
forth, in perfect time to the rattle of the gragger,
until all that was visible was a great gremlin
blur. Then, all of a sudden, from within that
blur, came a poof, then another and another, as
gremlin after vibrating gremlin shattered into a
large grey cloud of gremlin dust.

The gusty wind, which was somehow still
blowing, lifted the cloud of dust up into the
night sky and carried it away, over the gragger
house and far, far beyond. For a moment, the
cloud cast a shadow over the silvery moon.
Jacob strained his neck, staring up at the sky.
It was the strangest thing – maybe he was
dreaming, but the shadow looked exactly like
a wicked, frowning man wearing a triangle
shaped hat on his head. The man sneered down
at Purimville and raised a large, menacing fist.

But in the next moment, there was one final great gust of wind, and then the man was gone.

Jacob felt his legs drop to the ground, as the thunderous rattle of the gragger slowed to a dull boom, and then stopped altogether. He looked over at Poppy and Sarah, who were still clutching the gragger pole, both appearing as shaken up as he felt. They all took off their earmuffs, and for a brief moment, enjoyed the silence that once again hung over Purimville.

"We did it, Sarah," said Jacob, a satisfied grin slowly spreading across his face. "I think we have solved the Purimville problem!"

10

Farewell to Purimville

Do you think they're gone for good?" asked Poppy.

"I would guess they are," answered Sarah. "But if those gremlins ever do somehow come back, you'll know just how to get rid of them."

Suddenly, the silence of the night was broken by shuffling sounds coming from the other side of the gragger house. Jacob stiffened, listening carefully. Could it be the gremlins? Had they come back? Shadows moved around the gragger house towards them. And then, Jacob got a glimpse of what it was - the hamantashies, creeping cautiously and curiously, uncertain whether it was safe yet to come out.

"It's okay, hamantashies," called Jacob. "The gremlins are gone, and we don't think they'll be back any time soon!"

"It's true," chimed in Poppy, "Thanks to the brains and bravery of these two children – Jacob and Sarah."

There was a great deal of cheering all around, and then the hamantashies burst out in song and began to dance merrily in the light of the moon.

Poppy turned to Jacob and Sarah. "Come on. I have something to show you before you go."

She scurried to the costume factory, and Jacob and Sarah followed. Poppy threw open the door and stepped inside, exposing racks of colourful, sparkling costumes of every sort imaginable. Poppy dashed across the floor, and returned moments later with two bags. "I know that your costumes at home are all muddled, so here, please take these with you to wear on Purim." Poppy handed each of them a bag. "Open them when you're back," Poppy said. "And think of us here in Purimville when you wear them."

"We will, for sure," said Sarah. "Thanks, Poppy." Poppy blinked away a small tear as the children pulled the golden graggers out of their pockets. Then, with the strains of the *Hamantash* song echoing in the background, they began to twirl their graggers. "Happy Purim!" they heard Poppy cry, just before golden sparks began to fly, and Purimville was left behind.

Moments later, back in Jacob's room, the children excitedly opened the bags that Poppy had given them. Inside were the best costumes that they had ever seen. For Sarah, there was a jester costume – a clown suit striped in purple and red, with golden bells on the hat that jingled the tune of *Hag Purim*. And for Jacob, there was a blue velvet cloak edged with gold, a handsome golden crown and a jewel handled sword that was somehow disguised as a scepter which sparkled as if it were magic.

Finally, at the very bottom of each bag the children found a gragger just like the one that had chased the gremlins from Purimville. These graggers were much smaller though, and while they made a nice loud sound, you didn't need earmuffs to use them.

Epilogue

The next evening, Jacob and Sarah sat in synagogue together to hear the story of Queen Esther being read for Purim. Sarah was there with her Uncle Solomon and Jacob was with his parents.

Both children were dressed up in their wonderful costumes and held graggers in their hands. They listened as the rabbi told of how brave Queen Esther saved the Jewish people from the wicked Haman. When Haman's name was mentioned,

Jacob and Sarah twirled their graggers and booed as loudly as they could, along with all of the other children and some of the grownups in the synagogue. For a moment, the noise reminded Jacob and Sarah of Purimville. They smiled at each other, and wondered what kind of marvelous adventure the next Jewish holiday might bring.

To read more about Purim, including fun recipes, ideas and information, go to www.jorabooks.com.